Books are to be returned on or before
the last date below.

1 9 OCT 2013

3 0 AUG 2016

1 1 MAR 2014

- 5 SEP 2014

1 1 DEC 2014

2 8 MAR 2017   4 JUL 2018

2 5 APR 2017

3 0 JAN 2015

2 1 AUG 2018
0 8 SEP 2018

1 2 MAY 2015   1 9 JUL 2017   1 3 OCT 2018

0 9 SEP 2017

3 0 MAR 2019

2 7 JUN 2015

1 5 AUG 2019

0 7 OCT 2017   1 5 MAR 2022

2 4 AUG 2015   1 2 DEC 2017

1 5 SEP 2015

1 4 NOV 2015   2 1 APR 2018

2 3 MAY 2016   1 9 MAR 2019

This book must be returned by the last date stamped above.
Rhaid dychwelyd y llyfr hwn erbyn y dyddiad diwethaf a stampiwyd uchod.

A charge will be made for any lost, damaged or overdue books.
Codir tâl os bydd llyfr wedi ei golli neu ei ni weidio neu heb ei ddychwelyd
mewn pryd.

Har de har har har Avast, timbers Polly want a Arr Arr Arr Bury, y Scallywags Lookin' the deck Arr Arr Arr the plank Hoist the and give 'em a cheer ship and shore Into t

e salty dog Shiver me
racker Blow me down
r treasure, lad Booty
r loot Yo ho ho Swab
Swashbuckler Walkin'
ail Lift up yer mugs
Scurvy skull Plunder
e drink Arr Arr Arr

Pirate Pete's
TALK LIKE A PIRATE

Pirate Pete's
TALK LIKE A PIRATE

by **Kim Kennedy** *illustrated by* **Doug Kennedy**

Abrams Books for Young Readers, London

Pirate Pete had the most amazing ship ever to sail the high seas, but he needed a crew. Not any old crew would do, however.

"I needs me a pirate crew," Pete told his parrot. "And I know just where to find one: Rascal Island!"

"To Rascal Island we go!" cried the bird.

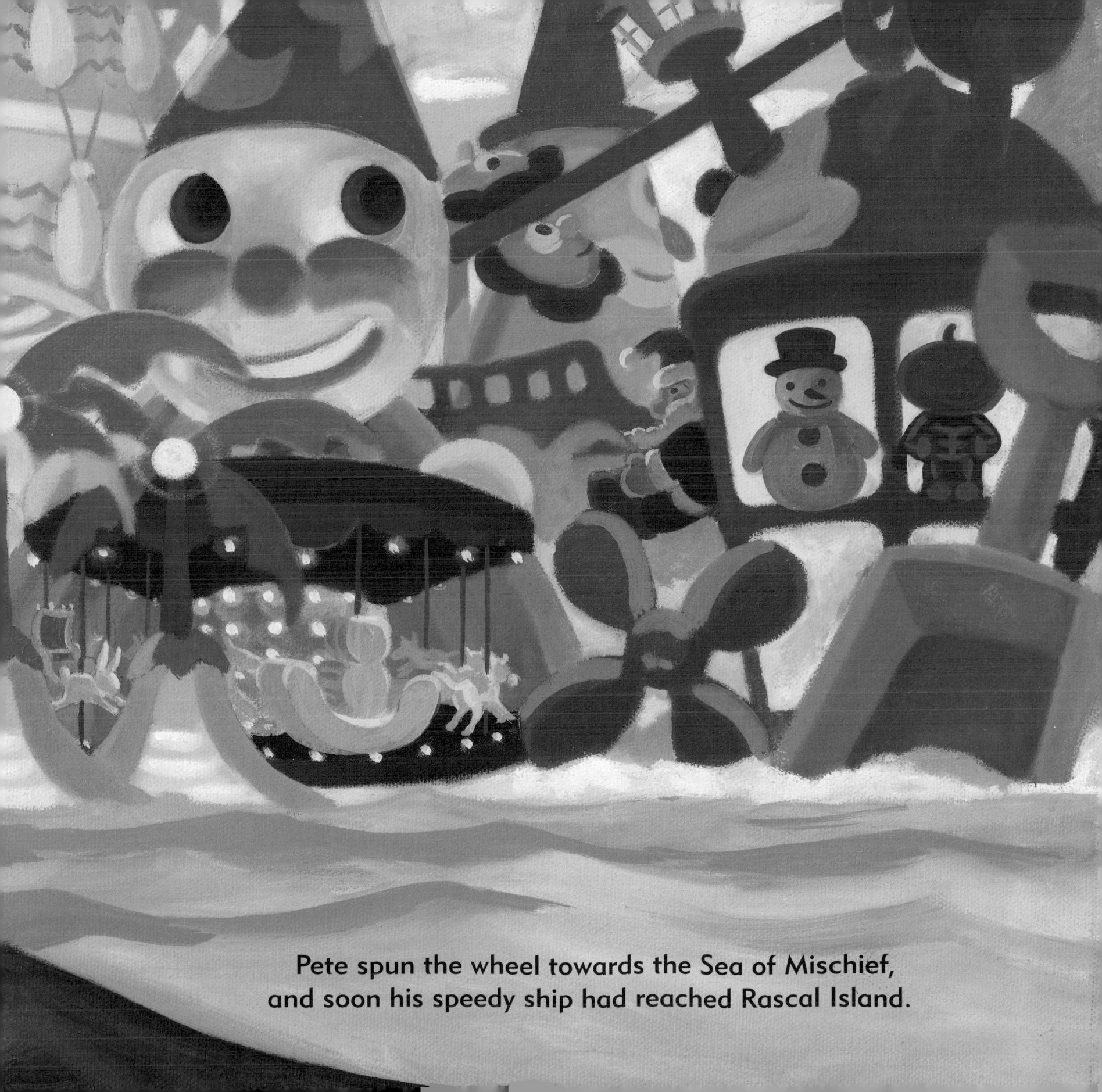

Pete spun the wheel towards the Sea of Mischief,
and soon his speedy ship had reached Rascal Island.

Pete dropped anchor in the bay, and then he hung
a sign across the ship's bow: BUCCANEERS WANTED.
Before long, a boat filled with rascals rowed up to
the ship. Pete rubbed his hands in glee! They were
the dirtiest, most mischievous, and sneakiest-looking
scallywags and scurvy dogs he'd ever laid his eye on.

One by one, the rascals climbed aboard the ship. "Listen up, mateys!" announced the parrot. "If ye wants to sail with Pete, then ye've gots to prove ye gots what it takes!"

Pete nodded and declared,
  "Ye needs a peg leg and an ol' eye patch,
  A fierce-lookin' hook and a beard ye can scratch!
  Ye gots to load a cannon and know how to fire it,
  But most of all, ye gots to talk like a pirate!"

A rascal stepped forward, loaded the cannon, and fired it.

"Nice firin'!" said Pete. "And I sees ye gots a peg leg, hook, and eye patch. And that beard of yours . . . does it hanker for a scratch?"

"It *is* quite itchy," answered the man. "Especially during the summer, when the weather tends to be sultry."

"Blow me down!" bellowed Pete. "Ye don't talk like a pirate! Walk the plank!"

As the man splashed overboard, Pete hollered,
"Ye should've said,
'When the sun's a-blazin',
Me beard gets the itches,
Worse than a bucket of sand down me britches!'"

"Next!" ordered the parrot.

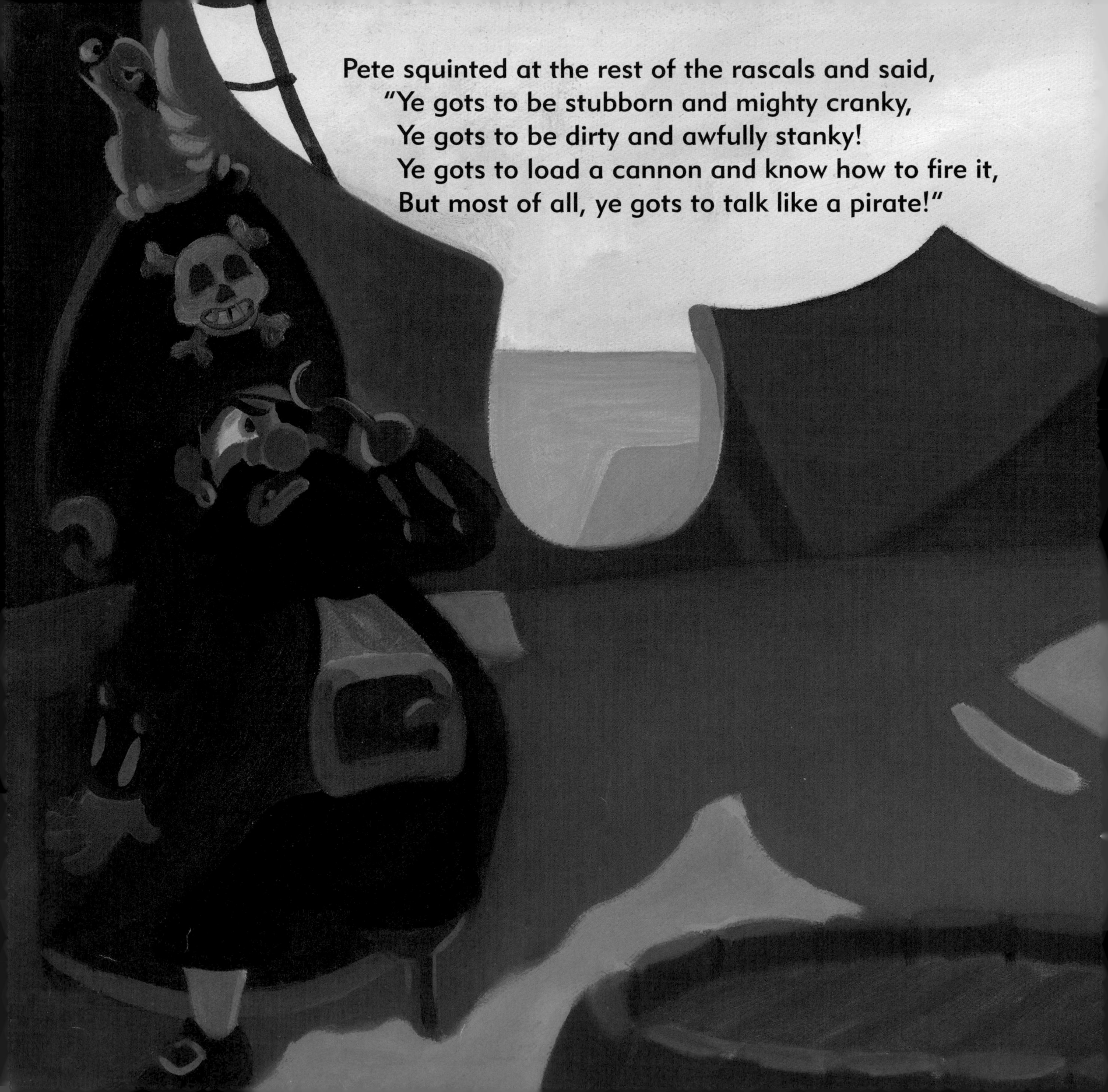

Pete squinted at the rest of the rascals and said,
"Ye gots to be stubborn and mighty cranky,
Ye gots to be dirty and awfully stanky!
Ye gots to load a cannon and know how to fire it,
But most of all, ye gots to talk like a pirate!"

A rascal stepped forward, loaded the cannon, and fired it.
"Nice firin'!" said Pete. "And I see that yer plenty dirty and stanky. But is ye stubborn and cranky?"

"Oh, indeed!" replied the rascal. "Sometimes I'm very irritable, especially when I don't eat my breakfast."

"Shiver me timbers!" shouted Pete. "Ye don't talk like a pirate! Walk the plank!"

As the rascal went overboard, Pete cried,
"Ye should've said,
       'I's as mean as a shark
       That's stuck in a tub,
       When I've not scarfed me mornin' grub!'"

"Next!" squawked the bird.

Pete glared at the rascals and said,
"Ye gots to love treasure! Why, it's your duty
To plunder ship and shore for gleamin' booty!
Ye gots to load a cannon and know how to fire it,
But most of all, ye gots to talk like a pirate!"

A rascal stepped forward, loaded the cannon, and fired it.

"Nice firin'!" said Pete. "And judgin' by the gold and rubies yer flauntin', I reckon ye've done some plunderin' in yer day."

"That is correct," said the rascal. "I've misappropriated a number of fine jewels without permission."

"Blimey!" cried Pete. "Ye don't talk like a pirate! Walk the plank!"

As the rascal leaped overboard, Pete shouted,
"Ye should've said,
   'I've pilfered loot on land and at sea,
   And no man's say-so has ever stopped me!'"

"Next!" blared the parrot.

Pete shook his head. He had finally lost his patience.
He curled up his lip at the last rascal and declared,
"Ye gots to trim the sails and mind the deck,
Ye gots to be brave in case of shipwreck,
Ye gots to load a cannon and know how to fire it,
But most of all, ye gots to talk like a pirate!"

The rascal walked forward, loaded the cannon, and fired it.

"Nice firin'!" said Pete. "But is ye brave? 'Cause no lily-livered seafarer is gonna sail with me!"

"I can *assure* you that I am extremely courageous," said the rascal. "I will conduct myself with valour at all times."

"Confound it!" shouted Pete, stomping his foot. "Ye don't talk like a pirate! Walk the plank!"

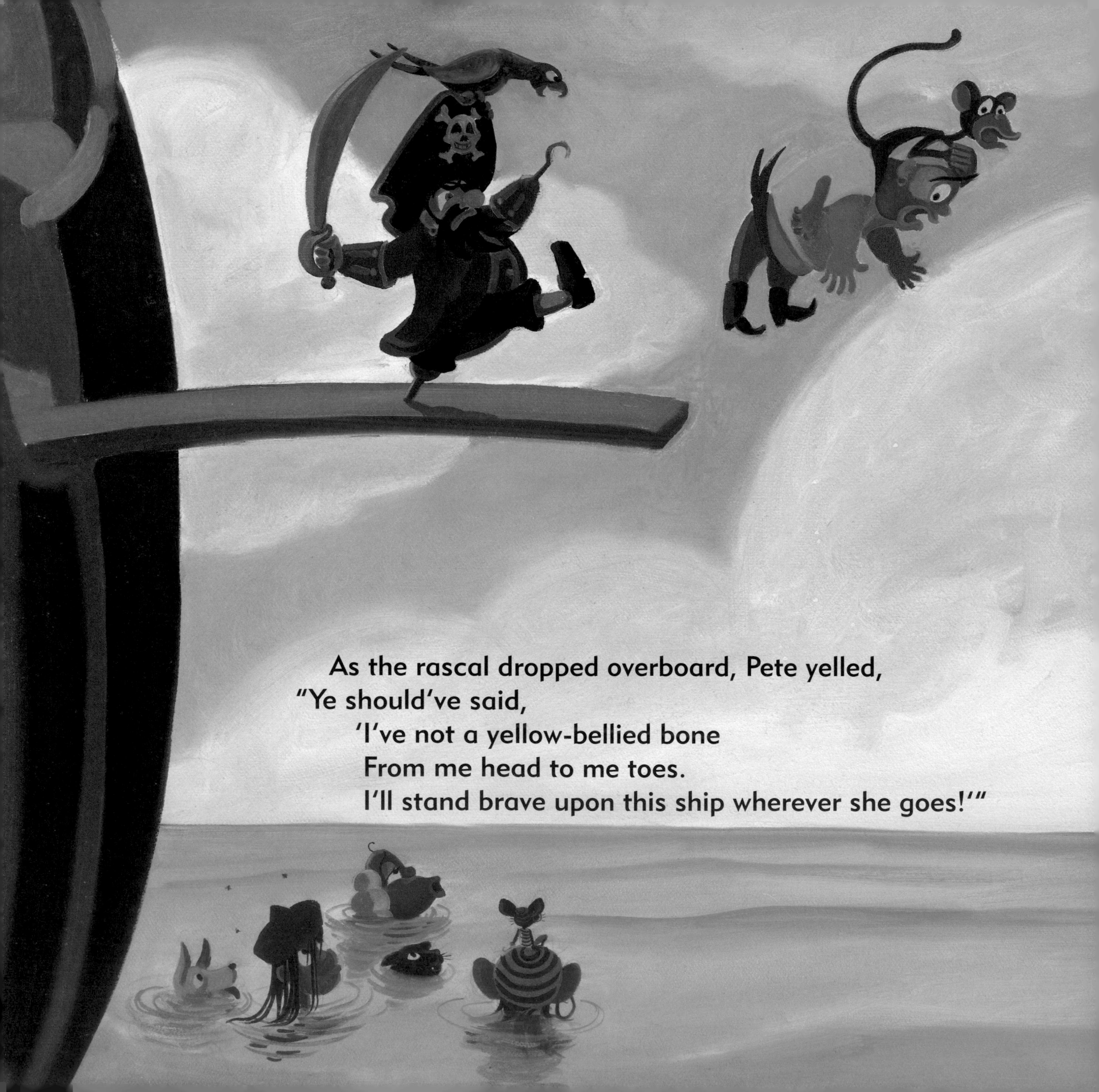

As the rascal dropped overboard, Pete yelled,
"Ye should've said,
   'I've not a yellow-bellied bone
   From me head to me toes.
   I'll stand brave upon this ship wherever she goes!'"

"Can ye believe it?" Pete moaned to his parrot. "Out of all them rascals, not a one was fit for me crew."

"'Tis true!" squawked the bird. "By the powers! They's no more than a bunch o' squiffies and sprogs! None of 'em fit to go a-swashbucklin' and plunderin' for pieces of eight upon the briney blue on this here vessel!"

Pete blinked.
"Why, ye talk just like a pirate!" he cheered to the bird. "Yer all the crew I needs. Weigh anchor!"

"Aye, aye," said the parrot, and off they sailed.

Back to the high seas went Pete and his bird.
A pirate always gets the last word!
They looked for a crew so they could hire it,
But blimey, none could talk like a pirate!

For Jackson
—Doug

For Dan
—Kim

The Library of Congress has catalogued the original edition of this book as follows:
Kennedy, Kim.
Pirate Pete's Talk Like a Pirate / by Kim Kennedy ; illustrated by Doug Kennedy.
p. cm.
Summary: In search of a crew, Pirate Pete and his parrot look for "stanky scallywags" who possess certain conversational skills.
ISBN: 978-0-8109-9348-8 (hc)
[1. Pirates—Fiction. 2. Parrots—Fiction.] I. Kennedy, Doug, ill. II. Title. III. Title: Talk like a pirate
PZ7.K3843Pg 2007
[E]—dc22
2006032066

ISBN for this edition: 978-0-8109-9757-8

Book design by Vivian Cheng

Printed and bound in China
10 9 8 7 6 5 4 3 2 1

Abrams Books for Young Readers are available at special discounts when purchased in quantity for premiums and promotions as well as fundraising or educational use. Special editions can also be created to specification. For details, contact specialmarkets@abramsbooks.com or the address below.

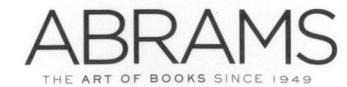

THE ART OF BOOKS SINCE 1949
The Market Building
72-82 Rosebery Avenue
London, UK EC1R 4RW
www.abramsbooks.co.uk

Har de har har har Avast,
timbers Polly want a
Arr Arr Arr Bury
Scallywags Lookin'
the deck Arr Arr Arr
the plank Hoist the
and give 'em a cheer
ship and shore Into

e salty dog Shiver me

racker Blow me down

r treasure, lad Booty

r loot Yo ho ho Swab

washbuckler Walkin'

ail Lift up yer mugs

curvy skull Plunder

e drink Arr Arr Arr

Har de har har har Avast,
timbers Polly want a
Arr Arr Arr Bury y
Scallywags Lookin'
the deck Arr Arr Arr
the plank Hoist the
and give 'em a cheer
ship and shore Into t